To my mom, Betty, for always encouraging
my magical thinking.
—R. W.

To Pat, Rudy, and Floyd.
Thank you for allowing me to stand atop your shoulders.
You are my inspiration, my motivation, and my family.
—X. Y.

FLAMINGO BOOKS
An imprint of Penguin Random House LLC, New York

First published in the United States of America by Flamingo Books, an imprint of Penguin Random House LLC, 2022

Visit us online at penguinrandomhouse.com.

Library of Congress Cataloging-in-Publication Data is available.

Printed in the United States of America

ISBN 9780593465882
10 9 8 7 6 5 4 3 2 1

WOR

Design by Nina Dunhill
Text set in Poppins

BUSY BETTY

by
Reese Witherspoon

illustrated by
Xindi Yan

FLAMINGO
BOOKS

Hi!
Hello!

Howdy!

I'm Betty!

I like DOING things

and MAKING things

and playing ALL day long!

Sweet cinnamon biscuits, I love being busy!

My big brother, Bo, says I've always been busy . . .

even when
I was a baby.

Turns out,
I was born busy!

My mom says, "Slow down, Betty! You have to focus to finish."

"Rome wasn't built in a day, Busy Betty," my dad says. "Hold your horses!"

"HORSeS?!?!?!

We don't have any horses!

But we do have the most
fantabulous dog in the entire universe!

"Whoa, Frank! YOU STINK!
What have you been rolling in? You're making my eyes water and my nose itch."

My tippity-top, numero-uno best friend, Mae, is coming soon, and I can't have a smelly dog at our playdate.

"I need to get busy and give you a bath!"

When my mom and I go to the pet store, I watch all the dogs get washed and brushed a hundred million times, so I'm basically a professional dog-washer anyway!

First things first,

I need a bathtub.

A pool is like a bathtub for outside!

"Betty . . . you can't wash a dog without soap," says Bo.

I guess Bo is right.
Well, I don't have soap,
but I do have . . .

BuBBLes!!

I love blowing bubbles!

Big, bouncy, beautiful bubbles.

I could blow a hundred billion bubbles a day!

Wait!
I have to *focus to finish.*

"Okay, Frank, jump through the Hula-Hoop, and the bubbles will get you squeaky-clean!"

Bouncing biscuits, how could I forget?

Frank never does tricks without a treat!
A treat like . . .

POPC⚬RN!

Frank will do almost anything for popcorn! And come to think of it, I'm kind of hungry.

"One for me, one for you . . . two for me,
two for you . . ."

"Betty," my dad calls, "Mae is on her way over!"
Uh-oh! We're getting messier
by the minute.

If you can't clean it, cover it!

A candy necklace for me
and a bow tie for Frank.

"Now, hold still, Frank, and don't knock over the . . ."

"Wait, Frank, come back!"

Busted biscuits, I've made a mess.

My mom will *see* this big mess, and she'll make me *clean* this big mess, and I won't get to play, because of this humongous, enormous, colossal, BIG MESS!

OH NOoo!!!

My playdate is RUINED.

Mae will be here any
minute, and she'll think this is . . .

"AMAZING!"

"Wow, Betty, look what you made!"

"WOW WHAT?? What *did* I make?" I ask Mae.

"You made a dog wash for Frank! What if we sold tickets to wash ALL the dogs on the block?"

I love Mae's idea! Time to get busy.

"When we pool our ideas,
we can do anything!"

"No time to hold our horses,
we've got to hold our hoses!"

"Together we will slide to success!"

"Betty!" Mae says. "We created a
bubble-blowing-dog-running-squeaky-
clean-canine-scrubbing . . ."

With my busy brain and Mae's perfect plan, we made a real-life dog-washing business!

Sweet cinnamon biscuits, we did it!
Being busy is a great way to be.

Right, Frank?